The Smoky God
Or
A Voyage to the Inner World

By Willis George Emerson

ISBN: 978-1-63118-423-9

Esoteric Classics:
Occult Fiction

Other Books in this Series and Related Titles

Magical Essays and Instructions by Florence Farr
(978-1-63118-418-5)

Ancient Mysteries and Secret Societies by Manly P. Hall
(978-1-63118-410-9)

The First and Second Gospels of the Infancy of Jesus Christ
by Thomas and James (978-1-63118-415-4)

The Human Aura: Astral Colors and Thought Forms
by Swami Panchadasi and William Walker Atkinson
(978-1-63118-419-2)

The Book of the Watchers by Enoch
(978-1-63118-416-1)

Thirty-One Hymns to the Star Goddess by Frater Achad
(978-1-63118-422-2)

Rosa Alchemica, The Tables of Law & The Adoration of the Magi
by William Butler Yeats (978-1-63118-421-5)

Occult Symbolism of Animals, Insects, Reptiles, Fish and Birds
by Manly P. Hall (978-1-63118-420-8)

The Lives of Adam and Eve by Moses (978-1-63118-414-7)

*A Collection of Writings Related to Occult, Esoteric, Rosicrucian and
Hermetic Literature, Including Freemasonry, the Kabbalah, the Tarot,
Alchemy and Theosophy* various authors *Volumes 1-4*
(978-1-63118-713-1) (978-1-63118-714-8)
(978-1-63118-715-5) (978-1-63118-716-2)

Audio Versions are also Available on Audible and iTunes

Table of Contents

Introduction

The word "esoteric" can be difficult to define. Esotericism in general can be seen less as a system of beliefs and more as a category, which encompasses numerous, different systems of beliefs. It's a bit of juxtaposition, since the word "esoteric" indicates something that few people know about, while the term itself broadly covers numerous philosophies, practices, areas of study and belief systems.

In a greater sense, Esotericism acts as a storehouse for secret knowledge, which is often considered ancient (by *tradition, if not by fact),* passed down from generation to generation, in private. At various times in history, simply possessing the knowledge of some of these subjects, was considered illegal and a jailable offence, if discovered. This usually included such general topics as Alchemy, Qabalah, Hermeticism, Occultism, Ceremonial Magic, Astrology, Divination, Rosicrucianism and so on. Collectively, these areas of study were often referred to as the esoteric sciences.

Sometimes, the outer garment of a subject isn't esoteric, while what is hidden beneath it, is. As an example, Freemasonry isn't necessarily esoteric by nature (at *least not anymore),* but certain signs, passwords and handshakes given to the candidate during their initiation, are in fact, esoteric, in the sense that they are hidden from the general public.

Today, in the twenty-first century, such topics are readily available at bookstores across the country, and numerous mainsteam publishers offer beginners guides and coffee-table volumes on many of these subjects, intended for mass appeal. Books like "*The Secret*" have turned previously arcane topics into household knowledge. All that being the case, however, it isn't to say that there still aren't buried secrets to uncover, ancient wisdom being ignored and forgotten mysteries to be explored. In fact, it is often that we are only able to further our own studies by standing on the shoulders of these disappearing giants.

Lamp of Trismegistus is doing its part to help preserve humanity's esoteric history by making some of these classics available to those students who are seeking to unearth the knowledge of these ancient colossi.

So, be sure to check other titles from our *Esoteric Classics* series, as well as our *Occult Fiction*, *Theosophical Classics*, *Foundations of Freemasonry* and our *Christian Apocrypha Series.*

Historical Introduction

Centuries after the general population stopped believing that the Earth was flat and years before YouTube celebrities and professional basketball players started believing that it was flat once again, there was a brief period of time, when *a few* people seemingly began to believe that the Earth was instead, hollow.

The idea of a hollow earth seems to have been first suggested in the late seventeenth century by Edmond Halley, of *Halley's Comet* fame. It's an idea that would give birth to a wide range of books and novels, over the centuries to come. While the scientific discoveries of the time, already existed to disprove the theory from a factual standpoint, the fantastical idea of a hollow Earth managed to hang on for quite a number of decades. Eventually, the genre of *subterranean literature* was born in 1741, to the first Hollow Earth novel. The writer was one Ludvig Holberg, and although the author was Norwegian himself, the novel was published in Latin.

The genre could have faded away just as easily as it arrived; however, it experienced an unexpected revival of interest, in the early nineteenth century, followed by an explosion in popularity with the publication of Jules Verne's 1864 novel, *Journey to the Center of the Earth.*

Sometimes literary trends can be traced to events, and this may be one of those situations. In the case of the unexpected popularity of the novel *Robinson Crusoe*, at the beginning of the eighteenth century, which spawned numerous immediate knock-offs and eventually an entire genre of *desert island literature*, it has been speculated that the popularity was tied to an increasing number of exploratory sea voyages. Prior to the discovery of the New World, all of Europe, the Mediterranean and other nearby lands had been thoroughly explored, mapped and documented. Any island capable of supporting life, was already established and had people thriving on it. The concept of finding a "new" island was not only absurd, it was an idea that nobody had thought to entertain. That changed, however, as sea faring vessels began regularly heading West on long journeys, only to return, or fail to return, months later. The fantasy of what sort of people and treasures might have been encountered and what sort of adventures took place, on an unknown island, was ripe for captivating story-telling.

A similar situation may have helped propel forward an interest in *subterranean literature*. This time, however, instead of voyages through warm island waters, it was exploration of the Northwest passage that began to receive heavy attention, during the middle to late nineteenth century, until the eventual discovery of the North Pole in 1909. While not all subterranean stories involve ice-locked passages, which eventually give way to a lush, green, Inner Earth, many of them do.

The concern, as the author states at the start of the book, is that the World's geography is incomplete. It is likely this driving notion that similarly propelled the popularity of both *desert island literature* and *subterranean literature*, alike.

In addition to Jules Verne's notable novel, the genre saw a boost due to novels from other popular authors such as Edgar Allen Poe, Sir Arthur Conan Doyle and Edgar Rice Burroughs.

Concurrently, the genre was receiving an unexpected boost from other writers, like Lord Edward Bulwer-Lytton, who were connecting the idea of an Inner Earth with the general teachings of spiritual and occult sciences, which were, themselves, at the beginning of their own revival, during this same time period. In these versions of the stories, there were often gigantic or angelic beings, who were spiritually advanced versions of humanity, or even the Ascended Masters themselves, often charged with watching over the rest of us. Sometimes these beings might simply possess advanced technology, while at other times they had access to advanced spiritual and parapsychological abilities. In some of these versions, entrances to underground caverns, leading to the Inner Earth, are guarded by a secret sect of Himalayan monks, who have been charged with protecting humanity's lost, occult knowledge (*which is seemingly common information in the Inner Earth*).

Eventually, in the mid twentieth century, the spiritual side of *subterranean literature* would become combined with the burgeoning genre of UFO abduction tales, and many of the early abduction stories, such as those published by Ray Palmer, involved being taken aboard a flying saucer, which then flew inside the Inner Earth.

As for the author, Willis George Emerson himself, only a handful of bibliographical clues seem to have survived. He was born in Iowa and in spite of being raised on a farm, managed to attend college, graduate from law school and become a well-travelled and successful newspaper man, lawyer and politician.

He appears to have been a Freemason and possibly a Rosicrucian, based on a few stray references and some carefully worded sentences in this and one other novel, intended to catch the eye of fellow initiates, as is part of the oral tradition.

Perhaps one of the more interesting aspects of his biography is that he founded a town in Wyoming, called Encampment, which enjoyed a brief surge in population at the end of the nineteenth century, due to a short-lived copper-rush. During this time period, Emerson owned and operated a large mining company in the town.

Apart from *The Smoky God*, Emerson mostly wrote cowboy novels taking place in what was then called the Middle West. At least one notable novel of his, *The Treasure of Hidden Valley*, featured characters traveling to his town of Encampment, Wyoming in hopes of getting rich from copper mining. Amusingly, he wasn't the only writer to pen a book about this. Colleague, fellow author and future state senator of Wyoming, Charles E. Winter, also wrote a novel which takes place in the town of Encampment, called *Grandon of Sierra*.

Following the end of the copper-rush and the dwindling population of the town of Encampment, Emerson set his sights West, making his way out to California in 1904, where he penned *The Smoky God*, which was originally serialized in a monthly periodical called *National Magazine*, out of Boston.

Emerson lived out his sunset years in Los Angles, eventually passing away in 1918, at the relatively young age of 62.

Within the *subterranean literature* genre, *The Smoky God* tends to lean less toward the spiritual and more toward the scientific; however, there are still subtle hints of the occult, which are undeniably present.

The novel is presented as the author *(Emerson himself)*, reading to the audience, the deathbed manuscript of a Norwegian explorer named Olaf Jensen, the central character in the story. In this way, Emerson was most certainly attempting to remove himself from the responsibility of having to defend the tale from a factual stand point, because, without a doubt he is offering the reader this account of Olaf Jensen as a nonfiction narrative.

In the original version of this book, the author included footnotes, quoting articles from various scientific periodicals as well as citations of travel journals, from different arctic expeditions of the time period, in order to help reinforce the legitimacy of his story. These citations, all rather dry and academic in nature, unintentionally served to slow down the narration and story-flow. As such, they have been removed from this version, in order to help enhance your reading experience.

The Smoky God

or

A Voyage to the Inner World

"He is the God who sits in the center, on the navel of the earth, and he is the interpreter of religion to all mankind."—Plato.

Part One:

Author's Foreword

I fear the seemingly incredible story which I am about to relate will be regarded as the result of a distorted intellect superinduced, possibly, by the glamour of unveiling a marvelous mystery, rather than a truthful record of the unparalleled experiences related by one Olaf Jansen, whose eloquent madness so appealed to my imagination that all thought of an analytical criticism has been effectually dispelled.

Marco Polo will doubtless shift uneasily in his grave at the strange story I am called upon to chronicle; a story as strange as a Munchausen tale. It is also incongruous that I, a disbeliever, should be the one to edit the story of Olaf Jansen, whose name is now for the first time given to the world, yet who must hereafter rank as one of the notables of earth.

I freely confess his statements admit of no rational analysis, but have to do with the profound mystery concerning the frozen North that for centuries has claimed the attention of scientists and laymen alike.

However much they are at variance with the cosmographical manuscripts of the past, these plain statements may be relied upon as a record of the things Olaf Jansen claims to have seen with his own eyes.

A hundred times I have asked myself whether it is possible that the world's geography is incomplete, and that the startling narrative of Olaf Jansen is predicated upon demonstrable facts. The reader may be able to answer these queries to his own satisfaction, however far the chronicler of this narrative may be from having reached a conviction. Yet sometimes even I am at a loss to know whether I have been led away from an abstract truth by the *ignes fatui* of a clever superstition, or whether heretofore accepted facts are, after all, founded upon falsity.

It may be that the true home of Apollo was not at Delphi, but in that older earth-center of which Plato speaks, where he says: "Apollo's real home is among the Hyperboreans, in a land of perpetual life, where mythology tells us two doves flying from the two opposite ends of the world met in this fair region, the home of Apollo. Indeed, according to Hecatæus, Leto, the mother of Apollo, was born on an island in the Arctic Ocean far beyond the North Wind."

It is not my intention to attempt a discussion of the theogony of the deities nor the cosmogony of the world. My simple duty is to enlighten the world concerning a heretofore unknown portion of the universe, as it was seen and described by the old Norseman, Olaf Jansen.

Interest in northern research is international. Eleven nations are engaged in, or have contributed to, the perilous work of trying to solve Earth's one remaining cosmological mystery.

There is a saying, ancient as the hills, that "truth is stranger than fiction," and in a most startling manner has this axiom been brought home to me within the last fortnight.

It was just two o'clock in the morning when I was aroused from a restful sleep by the vigorous ringing of my door-bell. The untimely disturber proved to be a messenger bearing a note, scrawled almost to the point of illegibility, from an old Norseman by the name of Olaf Jansen. After much deciphering, I made out the writing, which simply said: "Am ill unto death. Come." The call was imperative, and I lost no time in making ready to comply.

Perhaps I may as well explain here that Olaf Jansen, a man who quite recently celebrated his ninety-fifth birthday, has for the last half-dozen years been living alone in an unpretentious bungalow out Glendale way, a short distance from the business district of Los Angeles, California.

It was less than two years ago, while out walking one afternoon, that I was attracted by Olaf Jansen's house and its homelike surroundings, toward its owner and occupant, whom I afterward came to know as a believer in the ancient worship of Odin and Thor.

There was a gentleness in his face, and a kindly expression in the keenly alert gray eyes of this man who had lived more than four-score years and ten; and, withal, a sense of loneliness that appealed to my sympathy. Slightly stooped, and with his hands clasped behind him, he walked back and forth with slow and measured tread, that day when first we met. I can hardly say what particular motive impelled me to pause in my walk and engage him in conversation. He seemed pleased when I complimented him on the attractiveness of his bungalow, and on the well-tended vines and flowers clustering in profusion over its windows, roof and wide piazza.

I soon discovered that my new acquaintance was no ordinary person, but one profound and learned to a remarkable degree; a man who, in the later years of his long life, had dug deeply into books and become strong in the power of meditative silence.

I encouraged him to talk, and soon gathered that he had resided only six or seven years in Southern California, but had passed the dozen years prior in one of the middle Eastern states. Before that he had been a fisherman off the coast of Norway, in the region of the Lofoden Islands, from whence he had made trips still farther north to Spitzbergen and even to Franz Josef Land.

When I started to take my leave, he seemed reluctant to have me go, and asked me to come again. Although at the time I thought nothing of it, I remember now that he made a peculiar remark as I extended my hand in leave-taking. "You will come again?" he asked. "Yes, you will come again someday. I am sure you will; and I shall show you my library and tell you many things of which you have never dreamed, things so wonderful that it may be you will not believe me."

I laughingly assured him that I would not only come again, but would be ready to believe whatever he might choose to tell me of his travels and adventures.

In the days that followed I became well acquainted with Olaf Jansen, and, little by little, he told me his story, so marvelous, that its very daring challenges reason and belief. The old Norseman always expressed himself with so much earnestness and sincerity that I became enthralled by his strange narrations.

Then came the messenger's call that night, and within the hour I was at Olaf Jansen's bungalow.

He was very impatient at the long wait, although after being summoned I had come immediately to his bedside.

"I must hasten," he exclaimed, while yet he held my hand in greeting. "I have much to tell you that you know not, and I will trust no one but you. I fully realize," he went on hurriedly, "that I shall not survive the night. The time has come to join my fathers in the great sleep."

I adjusted the pillows to make him more comfortable, and assured him I was glad to be able to serve him in any way possible, for I was beginning to realize the seriousness of his condition.

The lateness of the hour, the stillness of the surroundings, the uncanny feeling of being alone with the dying man, together with his weird story, all combined to make my heart beat fast and loud with a feeling for which I have no name. Indeed, there were many times that night by the old Norseman's couch, and there have been many times since, when a sensation rather than a conviction took possession of my very soul, and I seemed not only to believe in, but actually see, the strange lands, the strange people and the strange world of which he told, and to hear the mighty orchestral chorus of a thousand lusty voices.

For over two hours he seemed endowed with almost superhuman strength, talking rapidly, and to all appearances, rationally. Finally, he gave into my hands certain data, drawings and crude maps. "These," said he in conclusion, "I leave in your hands. If I can have your promise to give them to the world, I shall die happy, because I desire that people may know the truth, for then all mystery concerning the frozen Northland will be explained. There is no chance of your suffering the fate I suffered. They will not put you in irons, nor confine you in a mad-house, because you are not telling your own story, but mine, and I, thanks to the gods, Odin and Thor, will be in my grave, and so beyond the reach of disbelievers who would persecute."

Without a thought of the far-reaching results the promise entailed, or foreseeing the many sleepless nights which the obligation has since brought me, I gave my hand and with it a pledge to discharge faithfully his dying wish.

As the sun rose over the peaks of the San Jacinto, far to the eastward, the spirit of Olaf Jansen, the navigator, the explorer and worshiper of Odin and Thor, the man whose experiences and travels, as related, are without a parallel in all the world's history, passed away, and I was left alone with the dead.

And now, after having paid the last sad rites to this strange man from the Lofoden Islands, and the still farther "Northward Ho!", the courageous explorer of frozen regions, who in his declining years (after he had passed the four-score mark) had sought an asylum of restful peace in sun-favored California, I will undertake to make public his story.

But, first of all, let me indulge in one or two reflections:

Generation follows generation, and the traditions from the misty past are handed down from sire to son, but for some strange reason interest in the ice-locked unknown does not abate with the receding years, either in the minds of the ignorant or the tutored.

With each new generation a restless impulse stirs the hearts of men to capture the veiled citadel of the Arctic, the circle of silence, the land of glaciers, cold wastes of waters and winds that are strangely warm. Increasing interest is manifested in the mountainous icebergs, and marvelous speculations are indulged in concerning the earth's center of gravity, the cradle of the tides, where the whales have their nurseries, where the magnetic needle goes mad, where the Aurora Borealis illumines the night, and where brave and courageous spirits of every generation dare to venture and explore, defying the dangers of the "Farthest North."

One of the ablest works of recent years is "Paradise Found, or the Cradle of The Human Race at the North Pole," by William F. Warren. In his carefully prepared volume, Mr. Warren almost stubbed his toe against the real truth, but missed it seemingly by only a hair's breadth, if the old Norseman's revelation be true.

Dr. Orville Livingston Leech, scientist, in a recent article, says:

"The possibilities of a land inside the earth were first brought to my attention when I picked up a geode on the shores of the Great Lakes. The geode is a spherical and apparently solid stone, but when broken is found to be hollow and coated with crystals. The earth is only a larger form of a geode, and the law that created the geode in its hollow form undoubtedly fashioned the earth in the same way."

In presenting the theme of this almost incredible story, as told by Olaf Jansen, and supplemented by manuscript, maps and crude drawings entrusted to me, a fitting introduction is found in the following quotation:

"In the beginning God created the heaven and the earth, and the earth was without form and void." And also, "God created man in his own image." Therefore, even in things material, man must be God-like, because he is created in the likeness of the Father.

A man builds a house for himself and family. The porches or verandas are all without, and are secondary. The building is really constructed for the conveniences within.

Olaf Jansen makes the startling announcement through me, an humble instrument, that in like manner, God created the earth for the "within"—that is to say, for its lands, seas, rivers, mountains, forests and valleys, and for its other internal conveniences, while the outside surface of the earth is merely the veranda, the porch, where things grow by comparison but sparsely, like the lichen on the mountain side, clinging determinedly for bare existence.

Take an egg-shell, and from each end break out a piece as large as the end of this pencil. Extract its contents, and then you will have a perfect representation of Olaf Jansen's earth. The distance from the inside surface to the outside surface, according to him, is about three hundred miles. The center of gravity is not in the center of the earth, but in the center of the shell or crust; therefore, if the thickness of the earth's crust or shell is three hundred miles, the center of gravity is one hundred and fifty miles below the surface.

In their log-books Arctic explorers tell us of the dipping of the needle as the vessel sails in regions of the farthest north known. In reality, they are at the curve; on the edge of the shell, where gravity is geometrically increased, and while the electric current seemingly dashes off into space toward the phantom idea of the North Pole, yet this same electric current drops again and continues its course southward along the inside surface of the earth's crust.

In the appendix to his work, Captain Sabine gives an account of experiments to determine the acceleration of the pendulum in different latitudes. This appears to have resulted from the joint labor of Peary and Sabine. He says: "The accidental discovery that a pendulum on being removed from Paris to the neighborhood of the equator increased its time of vibration, gave the first step to our present knowledge that the polar axis of the globe is less than the equatorial; that the force of gravity at the surface of the earth increases progressively from the equator toward the poles."

According to Olaf Jansen, in the beginning this old world of ours was created solely for the "within" world, where are located the four great rivers—the Euphrates, the Pison, the Gihon and the Hiddekel. These same names of rivers, when applied to streams on the "outside" surface of the earth, are purely traditional from an antiquity beyond the memory of man.

On the top of a high mountain, near the fountain-head of these four rivers, Olaf Jansen, the Norseman, claims to have discovered the long-lost "Garden of Eden," the veritable navel of the earth, and to have spent over two years studying and reconnoitering in this marvelous "within" land, exuberant with stupendous plant life and abounding in giant animals; a land where the people live to be centuries old, after the order of Methuselah and other Biblical characters; a region where one-quarter of the "inner" surface is water and three-quarters land; where there are large oceans and many rivers and lakes; where the cities are superlative in construction and magnificence; where modes of transportation are as far in advance of ours as we with our boasted achievements are in advance of the inhabitants of "darkest Africa."

The distance directly across the space from inner surface to inner surface is about six hundred miles less than the recognized diameter of the earth. In the identical center of this vast vacuum is the seat of electricity—a mammoth ball of dull red fire—not startlingly brilliant, but surrounded by a white, mild, luminous cloud, giving out uniform warmth, and held in its place in the center of this internal space by the immutable law of gravitation. This electrical cloud is known to the people "within" as the abode of "The Smoky God." They believe it to be the throne of "The Most High."

Olaf Jansen reminded me of how, in the old college days, we were all familiar with the laboratory demonstrations of centrifugal motion, which clearly proved that, if the earth were a solid, the rapidity of its revolution upon its axis would tear it into a thousand fragments.

The old Norseman also maintained that from the farthest points of land on the islands of Spitzbergen and Franz Josef Land, flocks of geese may be seen annually flying still farther northward, just as the sailors and explorers record in their log-books. No scientist has yet been audacious enough to attempt to explain, even to his own satisfaction, toward what lands these winged fowls are guided by their subtle instinct. However, Olaf Jansen has given us a most reasonable explanation.

24

The presence of the open sea in the Northland is also explained. Olaf Jansen claims that the northern aperture, intake or hole, so to speak, is about fourteen hundred miles across. In connection with this, let us read what Explorer Nansen writes, on page 288 of his book: "I have never had such a splendid sail. On to the north, steadily north, with a good wind, as fast as steam and sail can take us, an open sea mile after mile, watch after watch, through these unknown regions, always clearer and clearer of ice, one might almost say: 'How long will it last 2' The eye always turns to the northward as one paces the bridge. It is gazing into the future. But there is always the same dark sky ahead which . means open sea." Again, the Norwood Review of England, in its issue of May 10, 1884, says: "We do not admit that there is ice up to the Pole—once inside the great ice barrier, a new world breaks upon the explorer, the climate is mild like that of England, and, afterward, balmy as the Greek Isles."

Some of the rivers "within," Olaf Jansen claims, are larger than our Mississippi and Amazon rivers combined, in point of volume of water carried; indeed their greatness is occasioned by their width and depth rather than their length, and it is at the mouths of these mighty rivers, as they flow northward and southward along the inside surface of the earth, that mammoth icebergs are found, some of them fifteen and twenty miles wide and from forty to one hundred miles in length.

Is it not strange that there has never been an iceberg encountered either in the Arctic or Antarctic Ocean that is not composed of fresh water? Modern scientists claim that freezing eliminates the salt, but Olaf Jansen claims differently.

Ancient Hindoo, Japanese and Chinese writings, as well as the hieroglyphics of the extinct races of the North American continent, all speak of the custom of sun-worshiping, and it is possible, in the startling light of Olaf Jansen's revelations, that the people of the inner world, lured away by glimpses of the sun as it shone upon the inner surface of the earth, either from the northern or the southern opening, became dissatisfied with "The Smoky God," the great pillar or mother cloud of electricity, and, weary of their continuously mild and pleasant atmosphere, followed the brighter light, and were finally led beyond the ice belt and scattered over the "outer" surface of the earth, through Asia, Europe, North America and, later, Africa, Australia and South America.

It is a notable fact that, as we approach the Equator, the stature of the human race grows less. But the Patagonians of South America are probably the only aborigines from the center of the earth who came out through the aperture usually designated as the South Pole, and they are called the giant race.

Olaf Jansen avers that, in the beginning, the world was created by the Great Architect of the Universe, so that man might dwell upon its "inside" surface, which has ever since been the habitation of the "chosen."

They who were driven out of the "Garden of Eden" brought their traditional history with them.

The history of the people living "within" contains a narrative suggesting the story of Noah and the ark with which we are familiar. He sailed away, as did Columbus, from a certain port, to a strange land he had heard of far to the northward, carrying with him all manner of beasts of the fields and fowls of the air, but was never heard of afterward.

On the northern boundaries of Alaska, and still more frequently on the Siberian coast, are found bone-yards containing tusks of ivory in quantities so great as to suggest the burying-places of antiquity. From Olaf Jansen's account, they have come from the great prolific animal life that abounds in the fields and forests and on the banks of numerous rivers of the Inner World. The materials were caught in the ocean currents, or were carried on ice-floes, and have accumulated like driftwood on the Siberian coast. This has been going on for ages, and hence these mysterious bone-yards.

On this subject William F. Warren, in his book already cited, pages 297 and 298, says: "The Arctic rocks tell of a lost Atlantis more wonderful than Plato's. The fossil ivory beds of Siberia excel everything of the kind in the world. From the days of Pliny, at least, they have constantly been undergoing exploitation, and still they are the chief headquarters of supply. The remains of mammoths are so abundant that, as Gratacap says, 'the northern islands of Siberia seem built up of crowded bones.' Another scientific writer, speaking of the islands of New Siberia, northward of the mouth of the River Lena, uses this language: 'Large quantities of ivory are dug out of the ground every year. Indeed, some of the islands are believed to be nothing but an accumulation of drift-timber and the bodies of mammoths and other antediluvian animals frozen together.' From this we may infer that, during the years that have elapsed since the Russian conquest of Siberia, useful tusks from more than twenty thousand mammoths have been collected."

But now for the story of Olaf Jansen. I give it in detail, as set down by himself in manuscript, and woven into the tale, just as he placed them, are certain quotations from recent works on Arctic exploration, showing how carefully the old Norseman compared with his own experiences those of other voyagers to the frozen North. Thus, wrote the disciple of Odin and Thor:

Part Two:

Olaf Jansen's Story

My name is Olaf Jansen. I am a Norwegian, although I was born in the little seafaring Russian town of Uleaborg, on the eastern coast of the Gulf of Bothnia, the northern arm of the Baltic Sea.

My parents were on a fishing cruise in the Gulf of Bothnia, and put into this Russian town of Uleaborg at the time of my birth, being the twenty-seventh day of October, 1811.

My father, Jens Jansen, was born at Rodwig on the Scandinavian coast, near the Lofoden Islands, but after marrying made his home at Stockholm, because my mother's people resided in that city. When seven years old, I began going with my father on his fishing trips along the Scandinavian coast.

Early in life I displayed an aptitude for books, and at the age of nine years was placed in a private school in Stockholm, remaining there until I was fourteen. After this I made regular trips with my father on all his fishing voyages.

My father was a man fully six feet three in height, and weighed over fifteen stone, a typical Norseman of the most rugged sort, and capable of more endurance than any other man I have ever known. He possessed the gentleness of a woman in tender little ways, yet his determination and will-power were beyond description. His will admitted of no defeat.

I was in my nineteenth year when we started on what proved to be our last trip as fishermen, and which resulted in the strange story that shall be given to the world,—but not until I have finished my earthly pilgrimage.

I dare not allow the facts as I know them to be published while I am living, for fear of further humiliation, confinement and suffering. First of all, I was put in irons by the captain of the whaling vessel that rescued me, for no other reason than that I told the truth about the marvelous discoveries made by my father and myself. But this was far from being the end of my tortures.

After four years and eight months' absence I reached Stockholm, only to find my mother had died the previous year, and the property left by my parents in the possession of my mother's people, but it was at once made over to me.

All might have been well, had I erased from my memory the story of our adventure and of my father's terrible death.

Finally, one day I told the story in detail to my uncle, Gustaf Osterlind, a man of considerable property, and urged him to fit out an expedition for me to make another voyage to the strange land.

At first I thought he favored my project. He seemed interested, and invited me to go before certain officials and explain to them, as I had to him, the story of our travels and discoveries. Imagine my disappointment and horror when, upon the conclusion of my narrative, certain papers were signed by my uncle, and, without warning, I found myself arrested and hurried away to dismal and fearful confinement in a madhouse, where I remained for twenty-eight years—long, tedious, frightful years of suffering!

I never ceased to assert my sanity, and to protest against the injustice of my confinement. Finally, on the seventeenth of

October, 1862, I was released. My uncle was dead, and the friends of my youth were now strangers. Indeed, a man over fifty years old, whose only known record is that of a madman, has no friends.

I was at a loss to know what to do for a living, but instinctively turned toward the harbor where fishing boats in great numbers were anchored, and within a week I had shipped with a fisherman by the name of Yan Hansen, who was starting on a long fishing cruise to the Lofoden Islands.

Here my earlier years of training proved of the very greatest advantage, especially in enabling me to make myself useful. This was but the beginning of other trips, and by frugal economy I was, in a few years, able to own a fishing-brig of my own.

For twenty-seven years thereafter I followed the sea as a fisherman, five years working for others, and the last twenty-two for myself.

During all these years I was a most diligent student of books, as well as a hard worker at my business, but I took great care not to mention to anyone the story concerning the discoveries made by my father and myself. Even at this late day I would be fearful of having any one see or know the things I am writing, and the records and maps I have in my keeping. When my days on earth are finished, I shall leave maps and records that will enlighten and, I hope, benefit mankind.

The memory of my long confinement with maniacs, and all the horrible anguish and sufferings are too vivid to warrant my taking further chances.

In 1889 I sold out my fishing boats, and found I had accumulated a fortune quite sufficient to keep me the remainder of my life. I then came to America.

For a dozen years my home was in Illinois, near Batavia, where I gathered most of the books in my present library, though I brought many choice volumes from Stockholm. Later, I came to Los Angeles, arriving here March 4, 1901. The date I well remember, as it was President McKinley's second inauguration day. I bought this humble home and determined, here in the privacy of my Own abode, sheltered by my own vine and fig-tree, and with my books about me, to make maps and drawings of the new lands we had discovered, and also to write the story in detail from the time my father and I left Stockholm until the tragic event that parted us in the Antarctic Ocean.

I well remember that we left Stockholm in our fishing-sloop on the third day of April, 1829, and sailed to the southward, leaving Gothland Island to the left and Oeland Island to the right. A few days later we succeeded in doubling Sandhommar Point, and made our way through the sound which separates Denmark from the Scandinavian coast. In due time we put in at the town of Christiansand, where we rested two days, and then started around the Scandinavian coast to the westward, bound for the Lofoden Islands.

My father was in high spirit, because of the excellent and gratifying returns he had received from our last catch by marketing at Stockholm, instead of selling at one of the seafaring towns along the Scandinavian coast. He was especially pleased with the sale of some ivory tusks that he had found on the west coast of Franz Joseph Land during one of his northern cruises the previous year, and he expressed the hope that this time we might again be fortunate enough to load our little fishing-sloop with ivory, instead of cod, herring, mackerel and salmon.

We put in at Hammerfest, latitude seventy-one degrees and forty minutes, for a few days' rest. Here we remained one week, laying in an extra supply of provisions and several casks of drinking-water, and then sailed toward Spitzbergen.

For the first few days we had an open sea and a favoring wind, and then we encountered much ice and many icebergs. A vessel larger than our little fishing-sloop could not possibly have threaded its way among the labyrinth of icebergs or squeezed through the barely open channels. These monster bergs presented an endless succession of crystal palaces, of massive cathedrals and fantastic mountain ranges, grim and sentinel-like, immovable as some towering cliff of solid rock, standing silent as a sphinx, resisting the restless waves of a fretful sea.

After many narrow escapes, we arrived at Spitzbergen on the 23d of June, and anchored at Wijade Bay for a short time, where we were quite successful in our catches. We then lifted anchor and sailed through the Hinlopen Strait, and coasted along the North-East-Land.

A strong wind came up from the southwest, and my father said that we had better take advantage of it and try to reach Franz Josef Land, where, the year before he had, by accident, found the ivory tusks that had brought him such a good price at Stockholm.

Never, before or since, have I seen so many sea-fowl; they were so numerous that they hid the rocks on the coast line and darkened the sky.

For several days we sailed along the rocky coast of Franz Josef Land. Finally, a favoring wind came up that enabled us to make the West Coast, and, after sailing twenty-four hours, we came to a beautiful inlet.

One could hardly believe it was the far Northland. The place was green with growing vegetation, and while the area did not comprise more than one or two acres, yet the air was warm and tranquil. It seemed to be at that point where the Gulf Stream's influence is most keenly felt.

On the east coast there were numerous icebergs, yet here we were in open water. Far to the west of us, however, were icepacks, and still farther to the westward the ice appeared like ranges of low hills. In front of us, and directly to the north, lay an open sea.

My father was an ardent believer in Odin and Thor, and had frequently told me they were gods who came from far beyond the "North Wind."

There was a tradition, my father explained, that still farther northward was a land more beautiful than any that mortal man had ever known, and that it was inhabited by the "Chosen."

My youthful imagination was fired by the ardor, zeal and religious fervor of, my good father, and I exclaimed: "Why not sail to this goodly land? The sky is fair, the wind favorable and the sea open."

Even now I can see the expression of pleasurable surprise on his countenance as he turned toward me and asked:

"My son, are you willing to go with me and explore—to go far beyond where man has ever ventured?" I answered affirmatively. "Very well," he replied. "May the god Odin protect us!" and, quickly adjusting the sails, he glanced at our compass, turned the prow in due northerly direction through an open channel, and our voyage had begun.

The sun was low in the horizon, as it was still the early summer. Indeed, we had almost four months of day ahead of us before the frozen night could come on again.

Our little fishing-sloop sprang forward as if eager as ourselves for adventure. Within thirty-six hours we were out of sight of the highest point on the coast line of Franz Josef Land. We seemed to be in a strong current running north by northeast. Far to the right and to the left of us were icebergs, but our little sloop bore down on the narrows and passed through channels and out into open seas—channels so narrow in places that, had our craft been other than small, we never could have gotten through.

On the third day we came to an island. Its shores were washed by an open sea. My father determined to land and explore for a day. This new land was destitute of timber, but we found a large accumulation of drift-wood on the northern shore. Some of the trunks of the trees were forty feet long and two feet in diameter.

After one day's exploration of the coast line of this island, we lifted anchor and turned our prow to the north in an open sea.

I remember that neither my father nor myself had tasted food for almost thirty hours. Perhaps this was because of the tension of excitement about our strange voyage in waters farther north, my father said, than anyone had ever before been. Active mentality had dulled the demands of the physical needs.

Instead of the cold being intense as we had anticipated, it was really warmer and more pleasant than it had been while in Hammerfest on the north coast of Norway, some six weeks before.

We both frankly admitted that we were very hungry, and forthwith I prepared a substantial meal from our well-stored larder. When we had partaken heartily of the repast, I told my father I believed I would sleep, as I was beginning to feel quite drowsy. "Very well," he replied, "I will keep the watch."

I have no way to determine how long I slept; I only know that I was rudely awakened by a terrible commotion of the sloop. To my surprise, I found my father sleeping soundly. I cried out lustily to him, and starting up, he sprang quickly to his feet. Indeed, had he not instantly clutched the rail, he would certainly have been thrown into the seething waves.

A fierce snow-storm was raging. The wind was directly astern, driving our sloop at a terrific speed, and was threatening every moment to capsize us. There was no time to lose, the sails had to be lowered immediately. Our boat was writhing in convulsions. A few icebergs we knew were on either side of us, but fortunately the channel was open directly to the north. But would it remain so? In front of us, girding the horizon from left to right, was a vaporish fog or mist, black as Egyptian night at the water's edge, and white like a steam-cloud toward the top, which was finally lost to view as it blended with the great white flakes of falling snow. Whether it covered a treacherous iceberg, or some other hidden obstacle against which our little sloop would dash and send us to a watery grave, or was merely the phenomenon of an Arctic fog, there was no way to determine.

By what miracle we escaped being dashed to utter destruction, I do not know. I remember our little craft creaked and groaned, as if its joints were breaking. It rocked and staggered to and fro as if clutched by some fierce undertow of whirlpool or maelstrom.

Fortunately, our compass had been fastened with long screws to a crossbeam. Most of our provisions, however, were tumbled out and swept away from the deck of the cuddy, and had we not taken the precaution at the very beginning to tie ourselves firmly to the masts of the sloop, we should have been swept into the lashing sea.

Above the deafening tumult of the raging waves, I heard my father's voice. "Be courageous, my son," he shouted, "Odin is the god of the waters, the companion of the brave, and he is with us. Fear not."

To me it seemed there was no possibility of our escaping a horrible death. The little sloop was shipping water, the snow was falling so fast as to be blinding, and the waves were tumbling over our counters in reckless white-sprayed fury. There was no telling what instant we should be dashed against some drifting ice-pack.

The tremendous swells would heave us up to the very peaks of mountainous waves, then plunge us down into the depths of the sea's trough as if our fishing-sloop were a fragile shell. Gigantic white-capped waves, like veritable walls, fenced us in, fore and aft.

This terrible nerve-racking ordeal, with its nameless horrors of suspense and agony of fear indescribable, continued for more than three hours, and all the time we were being driven forward at fierce speed. Then suddenly, as if growing weary of its frantic exertions, the wind began to lessen its fury and by degrees to die down.

At last we were in a perfect calm. The fog mist had also disappeared, and before us lay an iceless channel perhaps ten or fifteen miles wide, with a few icebergs far away to our right, and an intermittent archipelago of smaller ones to the left.

I watched my father closely, determined to remain silent until he spoke. Presently he untied the rope from his waist and, without saying a word, began working the pumps, which fortunately were not damaged, relieving the sloop of the water it had shipped in the madness of the storm.

He put up the sloop's sails as calmly as if casting a fishing-net, and then remarked that we were ready for a favoring wind when it came. His courage and persistence were truly remarkable.

On investigation we found less than one-third of our provisions remaining, while to our utter dismay, we discovered that our water-casks had been swept overboard during the violent plungings of our boat.

Two of our water-casks were in the main hold, but both were empty. We had a fair supply of food, but no fresh water. I realized at once the awfulness of our position. Presently I was seized with a consuming thirst. "It is indeed bad," remarked my father. "However, let us dry our bedraggled clothing, for we are soaked to the skin. Trust to the god Odin, my son. Do not give up hope."

The sun was beating down slantingly, as if we were in a southern latitude, instead of in the far Northland. It was swinging around, its orbit ever visible and rising higher and higher each day, frequently mist-covered, yet always peering through the lacework of clouds like some fretful eye of fate, guarding the mysterious Northland and jealously watching the pranks of man. Far to our right the rays decking the prisms of icebergs were gorgeous. Their reflections emitted flashes of garnet, of diamond, of sapphire. A pyrotechnic panorama of countless colors and shapes, while below could be seen the green-tinted sea, and above, the purple sky.

Part Three:

Beyond the North Wind

I tried to forget my thirst by busying myself with bringing up some food and an empty vessel from the hold. Reaching over the side-rail, I filled the vessel with water for the purpose of laving my hands and face. To my astonishment, when the water came in contact with my lips, I could taste no salt. I was startled by the discovery. "Father!" I fairly gasped, "the water, the water; it is fresh!" "What, Olaf?" exclaimed my father, glancing hastily around. "Surely you are mistaken. There is no land. You are going mad." "But taste it!" I cried.

And thus we made the discovery that the water was indeed fresh, absolutely so, without the least briny taste or even the suspicion of a salty flavor.

We forthwith filled our two remaining water-casks, and my father declared it was a heavenly dispensation of mercy from the gods Odin and Thor.

We were almost beside ourselves with joy, but hunger bade us end our enforced fast. Now that we had found fresh water in the open sea, what might we not expect in this strange latitude where ship had never before sailed and the splash of an oar had never been heard?

We had scarcely appeased our hunger when a breeze began filling the idle sails, and, glancing at the coin-pass, we found the northern point pressing hard against the glass.

In response to my surprise, my father said, "I have heard of this before; it is what they call the dipping of the needle."

We loosened the compass and turned it at right angles with the surface of the sea before its point would free itself from the glass and point according to unmolested attraction. It shifted uneasily, and seemed as unsteady as a drunken man, but finally pointed a course.

Before this we thought the wind was carrying us north by northwest, but, with the needle free, we discovered, if it could be relied upon, that we were sailing slightly north by northeast. Our course, however, was ever tending northward.

The sea was serenely smooth, with hardly a choppy wave, and the wind brisk and exhilarating. The sun's rays, while striking us aslant, furnished tranquil warmth. And thus time wore on day after day, and we found from the record in our log-book, we had been sailing eleven days since the storm in the open sea.

By strictest economy, our food was holding out fairly well, but beginning to run low. In the meantime, one of our casks of water had been exhausted, and my father said: "We will fill it again." But, to our dismay, we found the water was now as salt as in the region of the Lofoden Islands off the coast of Norway. This necessitated our being extremely careful of the remaining cask.

I found myself wanting to sleep much of the time; whether it was the effect of the exciting experience of sailing in unknown waters, or the relaxation from the awful excitement incident to our adventure in a storm at sea, or due to want of food, I could not say.

I frequently lay down on the bunker of our little sloop, and looked far up into the blue dome of the sky; and, notwithstanding the sun was shining far away in the east, I always saw a single star overhead. For several days, when I looked for this star, it was always there directly above us.

It was now, according to our reckoning, about the first of August. The sun was high in the heavens, and was so bright that I could no longer see the one lone star that attracted my attention a few days earlier.

One day about this time, my father startled me by calling my attention to a novel sight far in front of us, almost at the horizon. "It is a mock sun," exclaimed my father. "I have read of them; it is called a reflection or mirage. It will soon pass away."

But this dull-red, false sun, as we supposed it to be, did not pass away for several hours; and while we were unconscious of its emitting any rays of light, still there was no time thereafter when we could not sweep the horizon in front and locate the illumination of the so-called false sun, during a period of at least twelve hours out of every twenty-four.

Clouds and mists would at times almost, but never entirely, hide its location. Gradually it seemed to climb higher in the horizon of the uncertain purply sky as we advanced.

It could hardly be said to resemble the sun, except in its circular shape, and when not obscured by clouds or the ocean mists, it had a hazy-red, bronzed appearance, which would change to a white light like a luminous cloud, as if reflecting some greater light beyond.

We finally agreed in our discussion of this smoky furnace-colored sun, that, whatever the cause of the phenomenon, it was not a reflection of our sun, but a planet of some sort—a reality.

One day soon after this, I felt exceedingly drowsy, and fell into a sound sleep. But it seemed that I was almost immediately aroused by my father's vigorous shaking of me by the shoulder and saying: "Olaf, awaken; there is land in sight!"

I sprang to my feet, and oh! joy unspeakable! There, far in the distance, yet directly in our path, were lands jutting boldly into the sea. The shore-line stretched far away to the right of us, as far as the eye could see, and all along the sandy beach were waves breaking into choppy foam, receding, then going forward again, ever chanting in monotonous thunder tones the song of the deep. The banks were covered with trees and vegetation.

I cannot express my feeling of exultation at this discovery. My father stood motionless, with his hand on the tiller, looking straight ahead, pouring out his heart in thankful prayer and thanksgiving to the gods Odin and Thor.

In the meantime, a net which we found in the stowage had been cast, and we caught a few fish that materially added to our dwindling stock of provisions.

The compass, which we had fastened back in its place, in fear of another storm, was still pointing due north, and moving on its pivot, just as it had at Stockholm. The dipping of the needle had ceased. What could this mean? Then, too, our many days of sailing had certainly carried us far past the North Pole. And yet the needle continued to point north. We were sorely perplexed, for surely our direction was now south.

We sailed for three days along the shoreline, then came to the mouth of a fjord or river of immense size. It seemed more like a great bay, and into this we turned our fishing-craft, the direction being slightly northeast of south. By the assistance of a fretful wind that came to our aid about twelve hours out of every twenty-four, we continued to make our way inland, into what afterward proved to be a mighty river, and which we learned was called by the inhabitants Hiddekel.

We continued our journey for ten days thereafter, and found we had fortunately attained a distance inland where ocean tides no longer affected the water, which had become fresh.

The discovery came none too soon, for our remaining cask of water was well-nigh exhausted. We lost no time in replenishing our casks, and continued to sail farther up the river when the wind was favorable.

Along the banks great forests miles in extent could be seen stretching away on the shore-line. The trees were of enormous size. We landed after anchoring near a sandy beach, and waded ashore, and were rewarded by finding a quantity of nuts that were very palatable and satisfying to hunger, and a welcome change from the monotony of our stock of provisions.

It was about the first of September, over five months, we calculated, since our leave-taking from Stockholm. Suddenly we were frightened almost out of our wits by hearing in the far distance the singing of people. Very soon thereafter we discovered a huge ship gliding down the river directly toward us. Those aboard were singing in one mighty chorus that, echoing from bank to bank, sounded like a thousand voices, filling the whole universe with quivering melody. The accompaniment was played on stringed instruments not unlike our harps.

It was a larger ship than any we bad ever seen, and was differently constructed.

At this particular time our sloop was becalmed, and not far from the shore. The bank of the river, covered with mammoth trees, rose up several hundred feet in beautiful fashion. We seemed to be on the edge of some primeval forest that doubtless stretched far inland.

The immense craft paused, and almost immediately a boat was lowered and six men of gigantic stature rowed to our little fishing-sloop. They spoke to us in a strange language. We knew from their manner, however, that they were not unfriendly. They talked a great deal among themselves, and one of them laughed immoderately, as though in finding us a queer discovery had been made. One of them spied our compass, and it seemed to interest them more than any other part of our sloop.

Finally, the leader motioned as if to ask whether we were willing to leave our craft to go on board their ship. "What say you, my son?" asked my father. "They cannot do any more than kill us."

"They seem to be kindly disposed," I replied, "although what terrible giants! They must be the select six of the kingdom's crack regiment. Just look at their great size."

"We may as well go willingly as be taken by force," said my father, smiling, "for they are certainly able to capture us." Thereupon he made known, by signs, that we were ready to accompany them.

Within a few minutes we were on board the ship, and half an hour later our little fishing-craft had been lifted bodily out of the water by a strange sort of hook and tackle, and set on board as a curiosity.

There were several hundred people on board this, to us, mammoth ship, which we discovered was called "The Naz," meaning, as we afterward learned, "Pleasure," or to give a more proper interpretation, "Pleasure Excursion" ship.

If my father and I were curiously observed by the ship's occupants, this strange race of giants offered us an equal amount of wonderment.

There was not a single man aboard who would not have measured fully twelve feet in height. They all wore full beards, not particularly long, but seemingly short-cropped. They had mild and beautiful faces, exceedingly fair, with ruddy complexions. The hair and beard of some were black, others sandy, and still others yellow. The captain, as we designated the dignitary in command of the great vessel, was fully a head taller than any of his companions. The women averaged from ten to eleven feet in height. Their features were especially regular and refined, while their complexion was of a most delicate tint heightened by a healthful glow.

Both men and women seemed to possess that particular ease of manner which we deem a sign of good breeding, and, notwithstanding their huge statures, there was nothing about them suggesting awkwardness. As I was a lad in only my nineteenth year, I was doubtless looked upon as a true Tom Thumb. My father's six feet three did not lift the top of his head above the waist line of these people.

Each one seemed to vie with the others in extending courtesies and showing kindness to us, but all laughed heartily, I remember, when they had to improvise chairs for my father and myself to sit at table. They were richly attired in a costume peculiar to themselves, and very attractive. The men were clothed in handsomely embroidered tunics of silk and satin and belted at the waist. They wore knee-breeches and stockings of a fine texture, while their feet were encased in sandals adorned with gold buckles. We early discovered that gold was one of the most common metals known, and that it was used extensively in decoration.

Strange as it may seem, neither my father nor myself felt the least bit of solicitude for our safety. "We have come into our own," my father said to me. "This is the fulfillment of the tradition told me by my father and my father's father, and still back for many generations of our race. This is, assuredly, the land beyond the North Wind."

We seemed to make such an impression on the party that we were given specially into the charge of one of the men, Jules Galdea, and his wife, for the purpose of being educated in their language; and we, on our part, were just as eager to learn as they were to instruct.

At the captain's command, the vessel was swung cleverly about, and began retracing its course up the river. The machinery, while noiseless, was very powerful.

The banks and trees on either side seemed to rush by. The ship's speed, at times, surpassed that of any railroad train on which I have ever ridden, even here in America. It was wonderful.

In the meantime we had lost sight of the sun's rays, but we found a radiance "within" emanating from the dull-red sun which had already attracted our attention, now giving out a white light seemingly from a cloud-bank far away in front of us. It dispensed a greater light, I should say, than two full moons on the clearest night.

In twelve hours this cloud of whiteness would pass out of sight as if eclipsed, and the twelve hours following corresponded with our night. We early learned that these strange people were worshipers of this great cloud of night. It was "The Smoky God" of the "Inner World."

The ship was equipped with a mode of illumination which I now presume was electricity, but neither my father nor myself were sufficiently skilled in mechanics to understand whence came the power to operate the ship, or to maintain the soft beautiful lights that answered the same purpose of our present methods of lighting the streets of our cities, our houses and places of business.

It must be remembered, the time of which I write was the autumn of 1829, and we of the "outside" surface of the earth knew nothing then, so to speak, of electricity.

The electrically surcharged condition of the air was a constant vitalizer. I never felt better in my life than during the two years my father and I sojourned on the inside of the earth.

To resume my narrative of events: The ship on which we were sailing came to a stop two days after we had been taken on board. My father said as nearly as he could judge, we were directly under Stockholm or London. The city we had reached was called "Jehu," signifying a seaport town. The houses were large and beautifully constructed, and quite uniform in appearance, yet without sameness. The principal occupation of the people appeared to be agriculture; the hillsides were covered with vineyards, while the valleys were devoted to the growing of grain.

I never saw such a display of gold. It was everywhere. The door-casings were inlaid and the tables were veneered with sheetings of gold. Domes of the public buildings were of gold. It was used most generously in the finishings of the great temples of music.

Vegetation grew in lavish exuberance, and fruit of all kinds possessed the most delicate flavor. Clusters of grapes four and five feet in length, each grape as large as an orange, and apples larger than a man's head typified the wonderful growth of all things on the "inside" of the earth.

The great redwood trees of California would be considered mere underbrush compared with the giant forest trees extending for miles and miles in all directions. In many directions along the foothills of the mountains vast herds of cattle were seen during the last day of our travel on the river.

We heard much of a city called "Eden," but were kept at "Jehu" for an entire year. By the end of that time we had learned to speak fairly well the language of this strange race of people. Our instructors, Jules Galdea and his wife, exhibited a patience that was truly commendable.

One day an envoy from the Ruler at "Eden" came to see us, and for two whole days my father and myself were put through a series of surprising questions. They wished to know from whence we came, what sort of people dwelt "without," what God we worshiped, our religious beliefs, the mode of living in our strange land, and a thousand other things.

50

The compass which we had brought with us attracted especial attention. My father and I commented between ourselves on the fact that the compass still pointed north, although we now knew that we had sailed over the curve or edge of the earth's aperture, and were far along southward on the "inside" surface of the earth's crust, which, according to my father's estimate and my own, is about three hundred miles in thickness from the "inside" to the "outside" surface. Relatively speaking, it is no thicker than an egg-shell, so that there is almost as much surface on the "inside" as on the "outside" of the earth.

The great luminous cloud or ball of dull-red fire—fiery-red in the mornings and evenings, and during the day giving off a beautiful white light, "The Smoky God,"—is seemingly suspended in the center of the great vacuum "within" the earth, and held to its place by the immutable law of gravitation, or a repellant atmospheric force, as the case may be. I refer to the known power that draws or repels with equal force in all directions.

The base of this electrical cloud or central luminary, the seat of the gods, is dark and non-transparent, save for innumerable small openings, seemingly in the bottom of the great support or altar of the Deity, upon which "The Smoky God" rests; and, the lights shining through these many openings twinkle at night in all their splendor, and seem to be stars, as natural as the stars we saw shining when in our home at Stockholm, excepting that they appear larger. "The Smoky God," therefore, with each daily revolution of the earth, appears to come up in the east and go down in the west, the same as does our sun on the external surface. In reality, the people "within" believe that "The Smoky God" is the throne of their Jehovah, and is stationary. The effect of night and day is, therefore, produced by the earth's daily rotation.

I have since discovered that the language of the people of the Inner World is much like the Sanskrit.

After we had given an account of ourselves to the emissaries from the central seat of government of the inner continent, and my father had, in his crude way, drawn maps, at their request, of the "outside" surface of the earth, showing the divisions of land and water, and giving the name of each of the continents, large islands and the oceans, we were taken overland to the city of "Eden," in a conveyance different from anything we have in Europe or America. This vehicle was doubtless some electrical contrivance. It was noiseless, and ran on a single iron rail in perfect balance. The trip was made at a very high rate of speed. We were carried up hills and down dales, across valleys and again along the sides of steep mountains, without any apparent attempt having been made to level the earth as we do for railroad tracks. The car seats were huge yet comfortable affairs, and very high above the floor of the car. On the top of each car were high geared fly wheels lying on their sides, which were so automatically adjusted that, as the speed of the car increased, the high speed of these fly wheels geometrically increased. Jules Galdea explained to us that these revolving fan-like wheels on top of the cars destroyed atmospheric pressure, or what is generally understood by the term gravitation, and with this force thus destroyed or rendered nugatory the car is as safe from falling to one side or the other from the single rail track as if it were in a vacuum; the fly wheels in their rapid revolutions destroying effectually the so-called power of gravitation, or the force of atmospheric pressure or whatever potent influence it may be that causes all unsupported things to fall downward to the earth's surface or to the nearest point of resistance.

The surprise of my father and myself was indescribable when, amid the regal magnificence of a spacious hall, we were finally brought before the Great High Priest, ruler over all the land. He was richly robed, and much taller than those about him, and could not have been less than fourteen or fifteen feet in height. The immense room in which we were received seemed finished in solid slabs of gold thickly studded with jewels of amazing brilliancy.

The city of "Eden" is located in what seems to be a beautiful valley, yet, in fact, it is on the loftiest mountain plateau of the Inner Continent, several thousand feet higher than any portion of the surrounding country. It is the most beautiful place I have ever beheld in all my travels. In this elevated garden all manner of fruits, vines, shrubs, trees, and flowers grow in riotous profusion.

In this garden four rivers have their source in a mighty artesian fountain. They divide and flow in four directions. This place is called by the inhabitants the "navel of the earth," or the beginning, "the cradle of the human race." The names of the rivers are the Euphrates, the Pison, the Gihon, and the Hiddekel.

The unexpected awaited us in this palace of beauty, in the finding of our little fishing-craft. It had been brought before the High Priest in perfect shape, just as it had been taken from the waters that day when it was loaded on board the ship by the people who discovered us on the river more than a year before.

We were given an audience of over two hours with this great dignitary, who seemed kindly disposed and considerate. He showed himself eagerly interested, asking us numerous questions, and invariably regarding things about which his emissaries had failed to inquire.

At the conclusion of the interview he inquired our pleasure, asking us whether we wished to remain in his country or if we preferred to return to the "outer" world, providing it were possible to make a successful return trip, across the frozen belt barriers that encircle both the northern and southern openings of the earth.

My father replied: "It would please me and my son to visit your country and see your people, your colleges and palaces of music and art, your great fields, your wonderful forests of timber; and after we have had this pleasurable privilege, we should like to try to return to our home on the 'outside' surface of the earth. This son is my only child, and my good wife will be weary awaiting our return."

"I fear you can never return," replied the Chief High Priest, "because the way is a most hazardous one. However, you shall visit the different countries with Jules Galdea as your escort, and be accorded every courtesy and kindness. Whenever you are ready to attempt a return voyage, I assure you that your boat which is here on exhibition shall be put in the waters of the river Heddekel at its mouth, and we will bid you Jehovah-speed."

Thus terminated our only interview with the High Priest or Ruler of the continent.

Part Four:

In the Underworld

We learned that the males do not marry before they are from seventy-five to one hundred years old, and that the age at which women enter wedlock is only a little less, and that both men and women frequently live to be from six to eight hundred years old, and in some instances much older.

During the following year we visited many villages and towns, prominent among them being the cities of Nigi, Delfi, Hectea, and my father was called upon no less than a half-dozen times to go over the maps which had been made from the rough sketches he had originally given of the divisions of land and water on the "outside" surface of the earth.

I remember hearing my father remark that the giant race of people in the land of "The Smoky God" had almost as accurate an idea of the geography of the "outside" surface of the earth as had the average college professor in Stockholm.

In our travels we came to a forest of gigantic trees, near the city of Delfi. Had the Bible said there were trees towering over three hundred feet in height, and more than thirty feet in diameter, growing in the Garden of Eden, the Ingersolls, the Tom Paines and Voltaires would doubtless have pronounced the statement a myth. Yet this is the description of the California *sequoia gigantea;* but these California giants pale into insignificance when compared with the forest Goliaths found in the "within" continent, where abound mighty trees from eight hundred to one thousand feet in height, and from one hundred to one hundred and twenty feet in diameter; countless in numbers and forming forests extending hundreds of miles back from the sea.

The people are exceedingly musical, and learned to a remarkable degree in their arts and sciences, especially geometry and astronomy. Their cities are equipped with vast palaces of music, where not infrequently as many as twenty-five thousand lusty voices of this giant race swell forth in mighty choruses of the most sublime symphonies.

The children are not supposed to attend institutions of learning before they are twenty years old. Then their school life begins and continues for thirty years, ten of which are uniformly devoted by both sexes to the study of music.

Their principal vocations are architecture, agriculture, horticulture, the raising of vast herds of cattle, and the building of conveyances peculiar to that country, for travel on land and water. By some device which I cannot explain, they hold communion with one another between the most distant parts of their country, on air currents.

All buildings are erected with special regard to strength, durability, beauty and symmetry, and with a style of architecture vastly more attractive to the eye than any I have ever observed elsewhere.

About three-fourths of the "inner" surface of the earth is land and about one-fourth water. There are numerous rivers of tremendous size, some flowing in a northerly direction and others southerly. Some of these rivers are thirty miles in width, and it is out of these vast waterways, at the extreme northern and southern parts of the "inside" surface of the earth, in regions where low temperatures are experienced, that freshwater icebergs are formed. They are then pushed out to sea like huge tongues of ice, by the abnormal freshets of turbulent waters that, twice every year, sweep everything before them.

We saw innumerable specimens of bird-life no less large than those encountered in the forests of Europe or America. It is well known that during the last few years whole species of birds have quit the earth. A writer in a recent article on this subject says:

Is it not possible that these disappearing bird species quit their habitation without, and find an asylum in the "within world"?

Whether inland among the mountains, or along the seashore, we found bird life prolific. When they spread their great wings some of the birds appeared to measure thirty feet from tip to tip. They are of great variety and many colors. We were permitted to climb up on the edge of a rock and examine a nest of eggs. There were five in the nest, each of which was at least two feet in length and fifteen inches in diameter.

After we had been in the city of Hectea about a week, Professor Galdea took us to an inlet, where we saw thousands of tortoises along the sandy shore. I hesitate to state the size of these great creatures. They were from twenty-five to thirty feet in length, from fifteen to twenty feet in width and fully seven feet in height. When one of them projected its head it had the appearance of some hideous sea monster.

The strange conditions "within" are favorable not only for vast meadows of luxuriant grasses, forests of giant trees, and all manner of vegetable life, but wonderful animal life as well.

One day we saw a great herd of elephants. There must have been five hundred of these thunder-throated monsters, with their restlessly waving trunks. They were tearing huge boughs from the trees and trampling smaller growth into dust like so much hazel-brush. They would average over 100 feet in length and from 75 to 85 in height.

It seemed, as I gazed upon this wonderful herd of giant elephants, that I was again living in the public library at Stockholm, where I had spent much time studying the wonders of the Miocene age. I was filled with mute astonishment, and my father was speechless with awe. He held my arm with a protecting grip, as if fearful harm would overtake us. We were two atoms in this great forest, and, fortunately, unobserved by this vast herd of elephants as they drifted on and away, following a leader as does a herd of sheep. They browsed from growing herbage which they encountered as they traveled, and now and again shook the firmament with their deep bellowing.

There is a hazy mist that goes up from the land each evening, and it invariably rains once every twenty-four hours. This great moisture and the invigorating electrical light and warmth account perhaps for the luxuriant vegetation, while the highly charged electrical air and the evenness of climatic conditions may have much to do with the giant growth and longevity of all animal life.

In places the level valleys stretched away for many miles in every direction. "The Smoky God," in its clear white light, looked calmly down. There was an intoxication in the electrically surcharged air that fanned the cheek as softly as a vanishing whisper. Nature chanted a lullaby in the faint murmur of winds whose breath was sweet with the fragrance of bud and blossom.

After having spent considerably more than a year in visiting several of the many cities of the "within" world and a great deal of intervening country, and more than two years had passed from the time we had been picked up by the great excursion ship on the river, we decided to cast our fortunes once more upon the sea, and endeavor to regain the "outside" surface of the earth.

We made known our wishes, and they were reluctantly but promptly followed. Our hosts gave my father, at his request, various maps showing the entire "inside" surface of the earth, its cities, oceans, seas, rivers, gulfs and bays. They also generously offered to give us all the bags of gold nuggets— some of them as large as a goose's egg—that we were willing to attempt to take with us in our little fishing-boat.

In due time we returned to Jehu, at which place we spent one month in fixing up and overhauling our little fishing sloop. After all was in readiness, the same ship "Naz" that originally discovered us, took us on board and sailed to the mouth of the river Hiddekel.

After our giant brothers had launched our little craft for us, they were most cordially regretful at parting, and evinced much solicitude for our safety. My father swore by the Gods Odin and Thor that he would surely return again within a year or two and pay them another visit. And thus we bade them adieu. We made ready and hoisted our sail, but there was little breeze. We were becalmed within an hour after our giant friends had left us and started on their return trip.

The winds were constantly blowing south, that is, they were blowing from the northern opening of the earth toward that which we knew to be south, but which, according to our compass's pointing finger, was directly north.

For three days we tried to sail, and to beat against the wind, but to no avail. Whereupon my father said: "My son, to return by the same route as we came in is impossible at this time of year. I wonder why we did not think of this before. We have been here almost two and a half years; therefore, this is the season when the sun is beginning to shine in at the southern opening of the earth. The long cold night is on in the Spitzbergen country."

"What shall we do?" I inquired.

"There is only one thing we can do," my father replied, "and that is to go south." Accordingly, he turned the craft about, gave it full reef, and started by the compass north but, in fact, directly south. The wind was strong, and we seemed to have struck a current that was running with remarkable swiftness in the same direction.

In just forty days we arrived at Delfi, a city we had visited in company with our guides Jules Galdea and his wife, near the mouth of the Gihon river. Here we stopped for two days, and were most hospitably entertained by the same people who had welcomed us on our former visit. We laid in some additional provisions and again set sail, following the needle due north.

On our outward trip we came through a narrow channel which appeared to be a separating body of water between two considerable bodies of land. There was a beautiful beach to our right, and we decided to reconnoiter. Casting anchor, we waded ashore to rest up for a day before continuing the outward hazardous undertaking. We built a fire and threw on some sticks of dry driftwood. While my father was walking along the shore, I prepared a tempting repast from supplies we had provided.

There was a mild, luminous light which my father said resulted from the sun shining in from the south aperture of the earth. That night we slept soundly, and awakened the next morning as refreshed as if we had been in our own beds at Stockholm.

After breakfast we started out on an inland tour of discovery, but had not gone far when we sighted some birds which we recognized at once as belonging to the penguin family. They are flightless birds, but excellent swimmers and tremendous in size, with white breast, short wings, black head, and long peaked bills. They stand fully nine feet high. They looked at us with little surprise, and presently waddled, rather than walked, toward the water, and swam away in a northerly direction.

The events that occurred during the following hundred or more days beggar description. We were on an open and iceless sea. The month we reckoned to be November or December, and we knew the so-called South Pole was turned toward the sun. Therefore, when passing out and away from the internal electrical light of "The Smoky God" and its genial warmth, we would be met by the light and warmth of the sun, shining in through the south opening of the earth. We were not mistaken.

There were times when our little craft, driven by wind that was continuous and persistent, shot through the waters like an arrow. Indeed, had we encountered a hidden rock or obstacle, our little vessel would have been crushed into kindling-wood.

At last we were conscious that the atmosphere was growing decidedly colder, and, a few days later, icebergs were sighted far to the left. My father argued, and correctly, that the winds which filled our sails came from the warm climate "within." The time of the year was certainly most auspicious for us to make our dash for the "outside" world and attempt to scud our fishing sloop through open channels of the frozen zone which surrounds the polar regions.

We were soon amid the ice-packs, and how our little craft got through the narrow channels and escaped being crushed I know not. The compass behaved in the same drunken and unreliable fashion in passing over the southern curve or edge of the earth's shell as it had done on our inbound trip at the northern entrance. It gyrated, dipped and seemed like a thing possessed.

One day as I was lazily looking over the sloop's side into the clear waters, my father shouted: "Breakers ahead!" Looking up, I saw through a lifting mist a white object that towered several hundred feet high, completely shutting off our advance. We lowered sail immediately, and none too soon. In a moment we found ourselves wedged between two monstrous icebergs. Each was crowding and grinding against its fellow mountain of ice. They were like two gods of war contending for supremacy. We were greatly alarmed. Indeed, we were between the lines of a battle royal; the sonorous thunder of the grinding ice was like the continued volleys of artillery. Blocks of ice larger than a house were frequently lifted up a hundred feet by the mighty force of lateral pressure; they would shudder and rock to and

62

fro for a few seconds, then come crashing down with a deafening roar, and disappear in the foaming waters. Thus, for more than two hours, the contest of the icy giants continued.

It seemed as if the end had come. The ice pressure was terrific, and while we were not caught in the dangerous part of the jam, and were safe for the time being, yet the heaving and rending of tons of ice as it fell splashing here and there into the watery depths filled us with shaking fear.

Finally, to our great joy, the grinding of the ice ceased, and within a few hours the great mass slowly divided, and, as if an act of Providence had been performed, right before us lay an open channel. Should we venture with our little craft into this opening? If the pressure came on again, our little sloop as well as ourselves would be crushed into nothingness. We decided to take the chance, and, accordingly, hoisted our sail to a favoring breeze, and soon started out like a race-horse, running the gauntlet of this unknown narrow channel of open water.

Part Five:

Among the Ice Packs

For the next forty-five days our time was employed in dodging icebergs and hunting channels; indeed, had we not been favored with a strong south wind and a small boat, I doubt if this story could have ever been given to the world.

At last, there came a morning when my father said: "My son, I think we are to see home. We are almost through the ice. See! the open water lies before us."

However, there were a few icebergs that had floated far northward into the open water still ahead of us on either side, stretching away for many miles. Directly in front of us, and by the compass, which had now righted itself, due north, there was an open sea.

"What a wonderful story we have to tell to the people of Stockholm," continued my father, while a look of pardonable elation lighted up his honest face. "And think of the gold nuggets stowed away in the hold!"

I spoke kind words of praise to my father, not alone for his fortitude and endurance, but also for his courageous daring as a discoverer, and for having made the voyage that now promised a successful end. I was grateful, too, that he had gathered the wealth of gold we were carrying home.

While congratulating ourselves on the goodly supply of provisions and water we still had on hand, and on the dangers we had escaped, we were startled by hearing a most terrific explosion, caused by the tearing apart of a huge mountain of ice. It was a deafening roar like the firing of a thousand cannons. We were sailing at the time with great speed, and happened to be near a monstrous iceberg which to all appearances was as immovable as a rockbound island. It seemed, however, that the iceberg had split and was breaking apart, whereupon the balance of the monster along which we were sailing was destroyed, and it began dipping from us. My father quickly anticipated the danger before I realized its awful possibilities. The iceberg extended down into the water many hundreds of feet, and, as it tipped over, the portion coming up out of the water caught our fishing-craft like a lever on a fulcrum, and threw it into the air as if it had been a foot-ball.

Our boat fell back on the iceberg, that by this time had changed the side next to us for the top. My father was still in the boat, having become entangled in the rigging, while I was thrown some twenty feet away.

I quickly scrambled to my feet and shouted to my father, who answered: "All is well." Just then a realization dawned upon me. Horror upon horror! The blood froze in my veins.

The iceberg was still in motion, and its great weight and force in toppling over would cause it to submerge temporarily. I fully realized what a sucking maelstrom it would produce amid the worlds of water on every side. They would rush into the depression in all their fury, like white-fanged wolves eager for human prey.

In this supreme moment of mental anguish, I remember glancing at our boat, which was lying on its side, and wondering if it could possibly right itself, and if my father could escape. Was this the end of our struggles and adventures? Was this death? All these questions flashed through my mind in the fraction of a second, and a moment later I was engaged in a life and death struggle. The ponderous monolith of ice sank below the surface, and the frigid waters gurgled around me in frenzied anger. I was in a saucer, with the waters pouring in on every side. A moment more and I lost consciousness.

When I partially recovered my senses, and roused from the swoon of a half-drowned man, I found myself wet, stiff, and almost frozen, lying on the iceberg. But there was no sign of my father or of our little fishing sloop. The monster berg had recovered itself, and, with its new balance, lifted its head perhaps fifty feet above the waves. The top of this island of ice was a plateau perhaps half an acre in extent.

I loved my father well, and was grief-stricken at the awfulness of his death. I railed at fate, that I, too, had not been permitted to sleep with him in the depths of the ocean. Finally, I climbed to my feet and looked about me. The purple-domed sky above, the shoreless green ocean beneath, and only an occasional iceberg discernible! My heart sank in hopeless despair. I cautiously picked my way across the berg toward the other side, hoping that our fishing craft had righted itself.

Dared I think it possible that my father still lived? It was but a ray of hope that flamed up in my heart. But the anticipation warmed my blood in my veins and started it rushing like some rare stimulant through every fiber of my body.

I crept close to the precipitous side of the iceberg, and peered far down, hoping, still hoping. Then I made a circle of the berg, scanning every foot of the way, and thus I kept going around and around. One part of my brain was certainly becoming maniacal, while the other part, I believe, and do to this day, was perfectly rational.

I was conscious of having made the circuit a dozen times, and while one part of my intelligence knew, in all reason, there was not a vestige of hope, yet some strange fascinating aberration bewitched and compelled me still to beguile myself with expectation. The other part of my brain seemed to tell me that while there was no possibility of my father being alive, yet, if I quit making the circuitous pilgrimage, if I paused for a single moment, it would be acknowledgment of defeat, and, should I do this, I felt that I should go mad. Thus, hour after hour I walked around and around, afraid to stop and rest, yet physically powerless to continue much longer. Oh! horror of horrors! to be cast away in this wide expanse of waters without food or drink, and only a treacherous iceberg for an abiding place. My heart sank within me, and all semblance of hope was fading into black despair.

Then the hand of the Deliverer was extended, and the death-like stillness of a solitude rapidly becoming unbearable was suddenly broken by the firing of a signal-gun. I looked up in startled amazement, when, I saw, less than a half-mile away, a whaling-vessel bearing down toward me with her sail full set.

Evidently my continued activity on the iceberg had attracted their attention. On drawing near, they put out a boat, and, descending cautiously to the water's edge, I was rescued, and a little later lifted on board the whaling-ship.

I found it was a Scotch whaler, "The Arlington." She had cleared from Dundee in September, and started immediately for the Antarctic, in search of whales. The captain, Angus MacPherson, seemed kindly disposed, but in matters of discipline, as I soon learned, possessed of an iron will. When I attempted to tell him that I had come from the "inside" of the earth, the captain and mate looked at each other, shook their heads, and insisted on my being put in a bunk under strict surveillance of the ship's physician.

I was very weak for want of food, and had not slept for many hours. However, after a few days' rest, I got up one morning and dressed myself without asking permission of the physician or anyone else, and told them that I was as sane as anyone.

The captain sent for me and again questioned me concerning where I had come from, and how I came to be alone on an iceberg in the far off Antarctic Ocean. I replied that I had just come from the "inside" of the earth, and proceeded to tell him how my father and myself had gone in by way of Spitzbergen, and come out by way of the South Pole country, whereupon I was put in irons. I afterward heard the captain tell the mate that I was as crazy as a March hare, and that I must remain in confinement until I was rational enough to give a truthful account of myself.

Finally, after much pleading and many promises, I was released from irons. I then and there decided to invent some story that would satisfy the captain, and never again refer to my trip to the land of "The Smoky God," at least until I was safe among friends.

Within a fortnight I was permitted to go about and take my place as one of the seamen. A little later the captain asked me for an explanation. I told him that my experience had been so horrible that I was fearful of my memory, and begged him to permit me to leave the question unanswered until sometime in the future. "I think you are recovering considerably," he said, "but you are not sane yet by a good deal." "Permit me to do such work as you may assign," I replied, "and if it does not compensate you sufficiently, I will pay you immediately after I reach Stockholm—to the last penny." Thus the matter rested.

On finally reaching Stockholm, as I have already related, I found that my good mother had gone to her reward more than a year before. I have also told how, later, the treachery of a relative landed me in a mad-house, where I remained for twenty-eight years—seemingly unending years—and, still later, after my release, how I returned to the life of a fisherman, following it sedulously for twenty-seven years, then how I came to America, and finally to Los Angeles, California. But all this can be of little interest to the reader. Indeed, it seems to me the climax of my wonderful travels and strange adventures was reached when the Scotch sailing-vessel took me from an iceberg on the Antarctic Ocean.

Part Six:

Conclusion

In concluding this history of my adventures, I wish to state that I firmly believe science is yet in its infancy concerning the cosmology of the earth. There is so much that is unaccounted for by the world's accepted knowledge of today, and will ever remain so until the land of "The Smoky God" is known and recognized by our geographers.

It is the land from whence came the great logs of cedar that have been found by explorers in open waters far over the northern edge of the earth's crust, and also the bodies of mammoths whose bones are found in vast beds on the Siberian coast.

Northern explorers have done much. Sir John Franklin, De Haven Grinnell, Sir John Murray, Kane, Melville, Hall, Nansen, Schwatka, Greely, Peary, Ross, Gerlache, Bernacchi, Andree, Amsden, Amundson and others have all been striving to storm the frozen citadel of mystery.

I firmly believe that Andree and his two brave companions, Strindberg and Fraenckell, who sailed away in the balloon "Oreon" from the northwest coast of Spitzbergen on that Sunday afternoon of July 11, 1897, are now in the "within" world, and doubtless are being entertained, as my father and myself were entertained by the kind-hearted giant race inhabiting the inner Atlantic Continent.

Having, in my humble way, devoted years to these problems, I am well acquainted with the accepted definitions of gravity, as well as the cause of the magnetic needle's attraction, and I am prepared to say that it is my firm belief that the magnetic needle is influenced solely by electric currents which completely envelop the earth like a garment, and that these electric currents in an endless circuit pass out of the southern end of the earth's cylindrical opening, diffusing and spreading themselves over all the "outside" surface, and rushing madly on in their course toward the North Pole. And while these currents seemingly dash off into space at the earth's curve or edge, yet they drop again to the "inside" surface and continue their way southward along the inside of the earth's crust, toward the opening of the so-called South Pole.

As to gravity, no one knows what it is, because it has not been determined whether it is atmospheric pressure that causes the apple to fall, or whether, 150 miles below the surface of the earth, supposedly one-half way through the earth's crust, there exists some powerful loadstone attraction that draws it. Therefore, whether the apple, when it leaves the limb of the tree, is drawn or impelled downward to the nearest point of resistance, is unknown to the students of physics.

Sir James Ross claimed to have discovered the magnetic pole at about seventy-four degrees latitude. This is wrong—the magnetic pole is exactly one-half the distance through the earth's crust. Thus, if the earth's crust is three hundred miles in thickness, which is the distance I estimate it to be, then the magnetic pole is undoubtedly one hundred and fifty miles below the surface of the earth, it matters not where the test is made. And at this particular point one hundred and fifty miles below the surface, gravity ceases, becomes neutralized; and when we pass beyond that point on toward the "inside" surface of the earth, a reverse attraction geometrically increases in power, until the other one hundred and fifty miles of distance is traversed, which would bring us out on the "inside" of the earth.

Thus, if a hole were bored down through the earth's crust at London, Paris, New York, Chicago, or Los-Angeles, a distance of three hundred miles, it would connect the two surfaces. While the inertia and momentum of a weight dropped in from the "outside" surface would carry it far past the magnetic center, yet, before reaching the "inside" surface of the earth it would gradually diminish in speed, after passing the halfway point, finally pause and immediately fall back toward the "outside" surface, and continue thus to oscillate, like the swinging of a pendulum with the power removed, until it would finally rest at the magnetic center, or at that particular point exactly one-half the distance between the "outside" surface and the "inside" surface of the earth.

The gyration of the earth in its daily act of whirling around in its spiral rotation—at a rate greater than one thousand miles every hour, or about seventeen miles per second—makes of it a vast electro-generating body, a huge machine, a mighty prototype of the puny-man-made dynamo, which, at best, is but a feeble imitation of nature's original.

The valleys of this inner Atlantis Continent, bordering the upper waters of the farthest north are in season covered with the most magnificent and luxuriant flowers. Not hundreds and thousands, but millions, of acres, from which the pollen or blossoms are carried far away in almost every direction by the earth's spiral gyrations and the agitation of the wind resulting therefrom, and it is these blossoms or pollen from the vast floral meadows "within" that produce the colored snows of the Arctic regions that have so mystified the northern explorers.

Beyond question, this new land "within" is the home, the cradle, of the human race, and viewed from the standpoint of the discoveries made by us, must of necessity have a most important bearing on all physical, paleontological, archaeological, philological and mythological theories of antiquity.

The same idea of going back to the land of mystery—to the very beginning—to the origin of man—is found in Egyptian traditions of the earlier terrestrial regions of the gods, heroes and men, from the historical fragments of Manetho, fully verified by the historical records taken from the more recent excavations of Pompeii as well as the traditions of the North American Indians.

-oOo-

It is now one hour past midnight—the new year of 1908 is here, and this is the third day thereof, and having at last finished the record of my strange travels and adventures I wish given to the world, I am ready, and even longing, for the peaceful rest which I am sure will follow life's trials and vicissitudes. I am old in years, and ripe both with adventures and sorrows, yet rich with the few friends I have cemented to me in my struggles to lead a just and upright life. Like a story that is well-nigh told, my life is ebbing away. The presentiment is strong within me that I shall not live to see the rising of another sun. Thus do I conclude my message.

Olaf Jansen.

74

Part Seven:

Author's Afterword

I found much difficulty in deciphering and editing the manuscripts of Olaf Jansen. However, I have taken the liberty of reconstructing only a very few expressions, and in doing this have in no way changed the spirit or meaning. Otherwise, the original text has neither been added to nor taken from.

It is impossible for me to express my opinion as to the value or reliability of the wonderful statements made by Olaf Jansen. The description here given of the strange lands and people visited by him, location of cities, the names and directions of rivers, and other information herein combined, conform in every way to the rough drawings given into my custody by this ancient Norseman, which drawings together with the manuscript it is my intention at some later date to give to the Smithsonian Institution, to preserve for the benefit of those interested in the mysteries of the "Farthest North" —the frozen circle of silence. It is certain there are many things in Vedic literature, in *"Josephus,"* the *"Odyssey,"* the *"Iliad,"* Terrien de Lacouperie's *"Early History of Chinese Civilization,"* Flammarion's *"Astronomical Myths,"* Lenormant's *"Beginnings of History,"* Hesiod's *"Theogony,"* Sir John de Maundeville's writings, and Sayce's *"Records of the Past,"* that, to say the least, are strangely in harmony with the seemingly incredible text found in the yellow manuscript of the old Norseman, Olaf Jansen, and now for the first time given to the world.

THE END

www.ingramcontent.com/pod-product-compliance
Lightning Source LLC
Chambersburg PA
CBHW051932240626
47153CB00004B/1466